The Dancing Colonel

by Lisa M. Lane

Grousable Books

This is a short story by Lisa M. Lane from *The Casebook of Inspector Slaughter and Friends*.

More information on her other books can be found at https://grousablebooks.com.

Published by Grousable Books
Encinitas, California
ISBN 979-8-9869845-8-2

"I do want you to help me, Jo, but you must dress."

Bridget adored her friend, but sometimes Jo was a little too insistent about her own comfort.

"You mean wear a crinoline? I don't even own one. And you've kindly hemmed up all my dresses."

Jo was an artist, and drew for *The Illustrated London News*, and yet, thought Bridget, she had no sense of style.

"Jo, the ball is my first chance to show that I can provide a full range of desserts. Everyone will be there, even Mrs. Beeton."

"Isabella Beeton, the cookery writer?"

Bridget nodded. "So you know how important this is."

Jo thought for a moment. Bridget had always wanted to be a pastry chef, but it had not been possible to train properly. She had been a photographer's assistant when she had inherited the shop in Theobalds Road, turned it into a bakery, and named it Cakes of

Distinction. Jo had been delighted for her, and very much wanted the business to succeed. But to wear a crinoline?

"Very well," she answered Bridget. "But you'll have to lend me one."

"Of course." Bridget smiled, her round cheeks dimpling prettily.

"And a dress."

"Ah," said Bridget. "Yes, all right, I'll let the hem out on my blue one for you."

The charity benefit ball for the Foundling Hospital was slated for Saturday. Mrs. Charles Fitzsimmons was the organizer, and she had happened upon Bridget's tea and cake shop with two friends she was trying to impress. Bridget's Madeira cake, a fluffy confection with lemon fondant, was both elegant and tasty, and Mrs. Fitzsimmons had forthwith hired Bridget for the ball.

The order was for eight cakes and three kinds of tarts. Bridget was grateful that she had hired an apprentice a few months ago. Jacques was only eighteen, but he was a quick learner, with a confidence that belied his age. But the job, particularly the set-up and serving, was too much for two people. Jo's efficiency and kindness would be most useful.

Since Cakes of Distinction had been open only two years, the shop had no van of its own, so Jacques borrowed one from the Porter and Sons bread bakery two streets away. Jo appeared at the shop at four o'clock, in proper dress, crinoline, and shawl, her dark hair looped over her ears. The three of them carefully loaded all of the confections into the back of the van. Jacques travelled in the back, his hands and feet stabilizing the boxes, while Bridget took the reins.

Willis's Rooms in St. James was a popular hall, available to let for various occasions. Several generations before it had been Almack's, a ballroom ruled by women at the pinnacle of society. It was said that in the 18th century the Duke of Wellington had been turned away for wearing trousers rather than breeches. Although such elegance had faded, the rooms were still splendid, with chandeliers and pilasters, a grand staircase, and two anterooms. The pastries and drinks were in one of these rooms, and when Bridget, Jo, and Jacques arrived the last two trestle tables were being covered with white tablecloths. Jo and Jacques worked under Bridget's direction, arraying the cakes and pastries. Mrs. Stevens came through, adding flower arrangements to the tables. The new colors meant rearranging many of the serving plates. Bridget's artistic sense demanded that the colors of the icings and flourishes, the carnation pinks and sunny yellows and deep reds, complement the floral arrangements.

Jacques returned to the van to chop the ice for the dishes that would keep everything cool until eight o'clock when the ball began. At seven they ate the food they had brought with them and watched the charity ladies set up the cloak room, lay out dance cards, and arrange for pitchers of water and a bowl of gin punch for thirsty dancers. The musicians arrived and prepared their platform. Two of the women stationed themselves near the door to collect tickets and provide information, including additional opportunities to donate to the Foundling Hospital.

Bridget noticed that several of the musicians looked very young, and she asked Jo about it.

"Perhaps they are protégés?"

Jacques came in with the ice and shook his head. He had been talking with the two young men setting up the drinks table.

"No. The Foundling Hospital has a band, to teach the young men music."

"Oh, that's delightful!" said Bridget, pleased to be taking part in such a worthy endeavor.

Soon the patrons began to arrive, and Jo was

amused as always by the bell-shaped skirts. The cage crinoline was beloved by women because it did away with heavy petticoats, replacing them with a single "cage" over which the skirt fabric lay. But the proportions, Jo felt, were now ridiculous, becoming so wide as to require tipping the skirt when passing through a doorway. This might reveal what was underneath, an utterly inappropriate thing to do. Architects had begun designing larger doorways to accommodate the trend, but Jo planned to wait until it passed.

Happily, the need to dance together in a crowded ballroom constrained the average skirt circumference. Even at its more modest proportions, however, Jo's crinoline made things difficult—it swung like it had a mind of its own, and she had to think before she turned herself too rapidly. She also knew that the sky blue color, which looked so charming on Bridget, did little to enhance her more forthright features.

Dancing began, as always, with a quadrille. Mrs. Beeton arrived, wearing a subdued gown of dove gray, and there was a flurry of greeting near the door. On the dance floor, partners turned and bowed to each other, then danced in step across the space, reaching out to touch hands, then turning together on the other side. After half an hour, committee members Mrs. Stevens and Mrs. Pole spoke from the band's platform, soliciting more donations by telling stories of particular foundling children who had done well. It was almost nine o'clock when Mrs. Fitzsimmons, a formidable matron with a black lace-covered gown and a necklace of black filigreed pearls to match, stood on the platform and raised her hands for silence.

"I hope everyone is enjoying the evening," she said in a voice one could only describe as operatic. "I would like to introduce you to two of the young men among our musicians this evening." She turned and motioned with her hand that they were to rise.

"Patrick O'Hara was found on the steps of St. Mary Moorfields and is now an excellent flute player and is apprenticed to a cobbler. Jimmy Hill was brought to our own hospital one night and, in addition to being a fine drummer, is learning French. Do give generously, everyone, to support the efforts of our Hospital in helping young men like these. And while you consider how much to give, please join us in the anteroom for refreshment. Our young men will serve the drinks, and our cakes are provided by Miss Bridget Williams of Cakes of Distinction."

By that point Bridget, Jo, and Jacques were at their

stations, ready to serve and suggest various delicacies. Patrick and Jimmy arrived to man the drinks table. For the next half hour there was continual activity, and Bridget was gratified to hear delighted murmurs when visitors saw her beautiful cakes or exclaimed at the excellent flavor. She had placed cards with the bakery's address scattered across the table, and some people were taking them. The famous Mrs. Isabella Beeton approached her table and Bridget had to suppress the impulse to curtsey.

"Mrs. Beeton," she said, nodding her head and smiling.

"Miss"—she glanced at the cards—"Williams. These look delightful. May I?"

Bridget served her a piece of cake, and was happy to see Mrs. Beeton smile as she took a bite.

"Quite delicious, my dear," she said, and Bridget felt herself blush. Several women heard her and each took one of Bridget's cards.

The mood in the anteroom was shifting gradually as the dancers returned to the main room and Patrick and Jimmy returned to the band. Jo could hear the strains of a waltz as they began to tidy up.

"Oh, may I go see them spin?" asked Jo. "I am working on a drawing and I want to see how close they are together." Bridget waved her away.

Jo watched the dancers, who were very close together, moving in a broad circle around the room. The hall was a hundred feet long but only forty feet wide, yet over twenty couples were on the floor. Jo watched how the dresses swung about, how the men's feet disappeared in the women's skirts (shocking!) and then appeared again, how still everyone kept their upper body. Some couples were laughing or talking, others intent and serious so that they didn't run into anyone.

The music changed and, amidst the laughter of the dancers, a polka began. Couples who had been gliding were now hopping together, circles within the bigger circle. The oom-pah oom-pah sound could be heard in the anteroom, and Bridget couldn't help tapping her feet as she began boxing up the remaining tarts. In the ballroom, Jo looked at the white-bearded man seated next to where she stood, and they exchanged a cheery smile as if to comment on the wildness of the polka.

Suddenly a gap opened in the circle, there was a shriek and a shuffling of feet, and the dancers stopped as they bumped into those who were now standing still. The musicians, assuming there had been an accident, stopped playing. There were cries for a doctor, and the old man next to Jo rose and moved swiftly toward the dance floor. Jo, following at his heels, heard murmurs that Colonel Marsh, poor man, had fallen into some kind of fit.

The Colonel was lying on the floor, and the doctor dropped to his knees, putting his ear to the Colonel's chest and a hand on his wrist. He then listened for breath, his ear just above the poor man's mouth. Jo noticed that the Colonel's face looked red and flushed; she saw that many dancers were pink from exertion. The doctor raised his head, looked around the room, and held up his hand.

"I'm sorry," he said. "I'm afraid Colonel Marsh has died."

There was a gasp, and the Colonel's dance partner, a young blonde woman who had been standing nearby, slid to the floor in a faint and was immediately attended by Mrs. Pole and Mrs. Stevens. A man brought a tablecloth from the anteroom and placed it over Colonel Marsh.

The commotion had brought Bridget and Jacques into the room.

"Should I fetch the police?" Jacques asked Bridget, who turned to him in silence, her eyes wide.

Jo heard him.

"It's been done," she said. "One man went to find a constable."

Mrs. Fitzsimmons, Mrs. Stevens, and Mrs. Pole were conferring in a corner. The band looked confused but had not left their seats, and some dancers were still standing on the dance floor while others had gone to find a place to sit. A few wandered into the anteroom. The constable and his beat sergeant arrived and began speaking with the dancers nearest the door. The sergeant went to talk with Mrs. Fitzsimmons as the constable kneeled to look under the tablecloth. Mrs. Fitzsimmons then stepped up onto the band platform.

"Your attention, if you please," she said. "As you can see, the police are here, and I'm afraid it would be unthinkable to continue our event this evening. Please, if you saw what happened on the floor, remain to describe what you saw to the sergeant and the constable. If you did not, and have no information that would be helpful, we ask you to return to your homes. We have names from the tickets and you may be called upon at a later time."

Many people collected their hats and coats, heading out into what had become a blustery chilly night. Jo began helping Bridget and Jacques put the cakes and pastries away, but the constable came in and asked them to stop, explaining that the sergeant would like them to remain on display for the time being. Patrick and Jimmy, back in the anteroom and beginning to clear the water pitchers and punch, were told the same. After a few minutes the doctor, who had already spoken to the police, came in and sat down in one of the chairs along the wall, giving Jo a rueful smile.

"I did not expect to work tonight," he said. "In fact, I retired over a year ago. But it seems a doctor's duty is never done."

Jo came over and sat next to him.

"Do you know what happened?" Jo asked him.

"I believe it was his heart giving out. Perhaps the vigorous dancing. Of course, he may have had a weak heart before, but that would be unlikely for a Colonel in an India regiment."

Bridget and Jacques came over, clearly wanting an introduction.

"I'm sorry," Jo said. "I'm afraid I don't know your name?"

The old gentleman smiled. "I'm Doctor Franks, retired physician and recently"—he apologetically looked at his stained fingers—"author of a medical textbook."

"I'm Jacques," said the young man, reaching out to

shake the man's hand. "And this is Bridget Williams, baker extraordinaire." The doctor nodded to Bridget.

"I'm Jo Harris," said Jo, holding up her own stained fingertips, "an artist for the *Illustrated London News*. Do you think the police would mind if I did some quick sketches?"

Doctor Franks shrugged. Jo excused herself, fetched her sketchpad from her satchel, and went into the ballroom.

"And do you know what the Colonel ate, drank, or smoked this evening?" the sergeant was asking the Colonel's dance partner, who was looking very pale and distraught.

"I only met him this evening, so I don't know what he might have had before he arrived," she said, dabbing her eyes with a handkerchief. "I think he had some punch earlier, and then pastries when we all went into the other room."

The police surgeon had arrived and was examining the poor colonel. Jo sat and sketched the body's shape under the tablecloth, the police surgeon and constable, and the unhappy dance partner. Jo was just focusing on the wood floor and the decorations on the walls when the sergeant approached her.

"May I ask what you are doing, ma'am?" His face

was placid, and his trim beard and moustaches showed an appreciation of order and control. But his voice was harsh and gravelly.

"I am an illustrator. I am sketching the scene."

The sergeant looked at her drawing.

"Very well done, ma'am. May I have your name please?"

"Jo Harris."

"Sergeant Collins. Did you know Colonel Marsh?"

"No, although I have heard of him. He was the one decorated for helping evacuate a group of British women and children from Agra during the mutinies, I believe."

"He was indeed. Did you speak with him this evening?"

"No, not at all." She pointed to the anteroom. "I was helping in there most of the time, although I came out to watch the waltz."

"The dance directly before the polka?"

"Yes."

The sergeant nodded as if this were meaningful information. "The refreshments were in there, you say?"

Jo followed him into the anteroom, where the sergeant introduced himself to Patrick and Jimmy at the drinks table.

"Did you see whether Colonel Marsh drank any water or punch?" asked the Sergeant.

The young men looked embarrassed.

"I'm sorry, but there were so many people in here," said Patrick. They could not say whether he had taken a drink among the crowds who came at the refreshment break, but didn't remember seeing him.

The sergeant asked Bridget's name.

"Bridget Williams, sergeant."

"Baker extraordinaire," added Jacques proudly. The sergeant looked over at him and frowned.

"Did either of you see Colonel Marsh take anything to eat from this table?"

Jacques shook his head, but Bridget nodded.

"He wanted a bit of several pastries and cakes. I gave him four different kinds. And," she said, glancing at the young men at the other table, "I did see he had a glass, and I think it was of punch."

"I see," said the sergeant. "Please wrap up one of each kind of pastry he had so I may take them for examination." Bridget began doing as he asked.

The constable entered the anteroom and came up to the sergeant.

"I have taken statements from the committee and

have told the band and all but Mrs. Fitzsimmons they may go. And," he said with a cautious look at the civilians, "I have information from the police surgeon."

Sergeant Collins accompanied the constable back into the ballroom, just inside the doorway, where they began speaking in earnest tones. Jacques, with a quick smile at Jo, sidled over to the small opening at the side of the door and listened, but shrugged when he could hear nothing.

Jo approached Sergeant Collins and handed him the wrapped pastries. "May we pack up now, please? Miss Williams is quite tired."

"I'm sorry, Miss Harris. We will be with you in a moment." The coroner's van was just arriving to collect Colonel Marsh's body.

Jo returned to Bridget and Jacques. The young dance partner followed, her eyes red, and asked Jimmy for a glass of water.

"I'm sorry, miss. I don't think that's a good idea."

"I suppose not," she sighed. She looked around at the others. "I just had to get out of that room. They are removing his—him—and I can't watch."

They nodded in sympathy.

"Your cakes were delicious," she said to Bridget. "I'm Esther Mayson, so I should know."

Bridget looked confused, then her face brightened. "Oh! Mrs. Beeton's sister. Well, you are welcome to stay in here with us."

She turned to the seats where Doctor Franks was sitting.

"Clearly the party is in here," he said with an ironic smile.

"Well, it's pretty dismal out there," said Jo. She turned to Esther. "Did you know Colonel Marsh?"

Esther shook her head, highlights glistening in her golden hair. "I just met him this evening. He sat next to me and began talking about India. All about the mutiny. I'm afraid I got a little bored," she said shyly. "So I asked him to dance, hoping I could excuse myself afterward."

Jo could imagine. Esther looked to be in her early twenties, and talk about an event that happened eight years ago could certainly seem tedious.

"Many dull stories came out of the mutiny," said Doctor Franks.

"Oh, now, Doctor, not that dull!" The police surgeon had come into the room, and was holding his hand out to Doctor Franks, who shook it heartily.

"Seamus! What on earth are you doing here?"

"Working, of course, Leopold."

"But I haven't seen you in years."

"Nor I you. How is the lovely Eugenie?"

Jo saw Doctor Franks' face change. "Gone only last year, Seamus. I thought you might have heard."

"My dear man, I had not. My sincerest condolences. She was a wonderful woman. And so brave. No one will ever forget what she did to get those women and children out of harm's way." He looked up and took notice of the others.

"My apologies," said Doctor Franks. Introductions were made all around.

"Can you tell us when they might permit us to go?" asked Bridget. "We didn't bring enough ice to keep these cakes fresh for so long."

Doctor MacDougall shook his head. "With only two policemen, this may take some time."

"But surely the cause was his heart, from the dancing?" asked Bridget.

MacDougall paused for a moment, as if assessing whether he should speak.

"I am of the opinion that he ingested poison here tonight, something that when combined with the dancing made his heart give out."

Bridget blanched.

"What's wrong?" asked Jo, putting her hand on

Bridget's elbow to steady her.

"The killer must have put something in my desserts," she said. "My business will be ruined."

"It could have been in the punch," Jacques said in a low voice, so Patrick and Jimmy couldn't hear.

"But the punch is in a bowl," Bridget pointed out. "It would have poisoned everyone who drank it."

Jo realized she had a point.

"Would you have seen if someone put something in the pastries?" asked Jo, her hand on her stomach as she recalled having eaten one of the treats earlier herself.

"Yes. I've been here the whole time. I would have seen."

"Then the killer was very prepared, and poisoned the food or drink before Colonel Marsh could consume it," said Jo. The two doctors nodded in agreement. "But why? Was the Colonel disliked?"

"Far from it," said MacDougall. "He was admired for his heroism during the mutiny. Not a dull story at all," he said, nodding to Doctor Franks. "He's in one of the paintings in the ballroom—did you see it?"

Jo was surprised at herself. She had spent little time looking at the paintings displayed high on the walls. "I would very much like to," she said.

MacDougall rose, bowed, and gave Jo his arm. The

others were content to remain in the anteroom.

The police were speaking with Mrs. Stevens, Mrs. Pole, and Mrs. Fitzsimmons. Dr. MacDougall escorted Jo to the side of the room and looked up.

"You can see there, the evacuation of Banáras. Marsh is the one on the left."

The painting showed a romanticized view of two women and three children being evacuated in a donkey cart, leaving a city whose smoke rose into the air behind them.

"They were escaping the rebellion?" Jo asked.

"Yes, it had just begun. The sepoys had risen up in several areas on both sides, and many families had left already. But as the mutiny spread, they had to escape by river, then travel many miles to the coast, where there were ships at Calcutta."

"And Marsh got them out?"

"He did, but many men were left behind and died."

MacDougall began to escort her back to the anteroom, but something caught Jo's eye. It was a round black ball, like an old bullet or an apothecary's pill. She picked it up, and returning to the anteroom saw another under the punch table. She sat down with the two beads in her hand.

"What did you find?" asked Bridget.

"These balls. I found them on the ground. They look like they're completely spherical, but they aren't."

She handed one to Bridget, who rolled it in her fingers.

"No, it isn't fully round. And it doesn't feel like a pearl or stone. It feels like"—she looked up at the ceiling as she thought—"candy. Like a hard sugar shell."

"Let's test it," said Jacques, who had joined them. "We could press it, or try to poke a hole in it."

"But it isn't ours," said Bridget. "It might be a pearl from a necklace."

"If it is," said Jo, "then no harm done."

"Even if it is an imitation pearl or stone, nothing we do can hurt it," Jacques pointed out.

Bridget set one down on the table and Jacques took up the cake knife. He pressed it with the side of the blade. It didn't give.

"Have you a hat-pin?" Jacques asked Jo, who shook her head.

"Oh! I have a sewing pin." She took one out of her pocket. Jacques pierced the side of the ball. Dark juice, so purple it was almost black, leaked out and soaked into the white tablecloth.

"Oh!" said Bridget, in surprise and annoyance. It didn't look like something easy to wash out of a tablecloth.

Dr. Franks came over to look.

"What have you there?"

Jo was perplexed. "I can't imagine what it could be."

Dr. Franks took a eyeglass out of his waistcoat pocket and examined the item.

"Seamus?" he said, calling MacDougall over. "What do you make of this?"

MacDougall peered at the object.

"If it weren't for the hard shell, I'd say—"

"Deadly nightshade," they both said together.

"The berries," Dr. Franks explained to Jo and Bridget, "are highly toxic, more so when they're fresh. These are fresh but coated in something to keep them that way."

"I'd say wax, perhaps?" said MacDougall. "Then likely lacquer for the hard shell."

"Did you see anyone wearing black beads?" asked Franks.

"I believe Mrs. Fitzsimmons is," said Jo. "I noticed them when we arrived."

"I'll be right back," said Jacques.

"Where are you going?" asked Jo.

"To make sure she's still wearing them." He swiftly made his way into the ballroom, and back almost as quickly.

"She doesn't have them," Jacques said. "She has a black lace kerchief instead."

Jo turned to Dr. Franks. "You said she lost her husband eight years ago?"

"Yes," said Franks. "He was in India. Left behind to defend Banáras. Murdered in horrible fashion by a rogue band taking advantage of the mutiny."

Jo, her eyes bright, then turned to Patrick and Jimmy. "Did either of you serve punch to Mrs. Fitzsimmons?"

Jimmy nodded. "Yes, she collected two glasses before the dancing began."

"So she could have put the poison in one of them, and given it to Colonel Marsh," said Jo. "No one would have noticed the color. Does it taste bitter?" she asked Dr. Franks.

"No, the fresh berries are quite sweet. Oh my Lord," said Dr. Franks, horrified. "Perhaps she blamed the colonel for not rescuing Major Fitzsimmons?"

"But that was years ago!" said Jacques.

"She's worn black ever since," said Franks. "Never came out of mourning."

Sergeant Collins came into the anteroom at that point, his constable trailing him with notebook in hand.

"We'll be continuing our investigation in the morning," Collins said. "Please give your address to my constable here, and we will contact you then."

"Sergeant Collins," said Jo. "That may not be necessary. We think we know what happened."

The group went into the ballroom to see Mrs. Fitzsimmons and the other women putting on their wraps, preparing to leave.

"Mrs. Fitzsimmons," said Jo. "I believe you are missing this?"

She held out the berry that was still intact. Mrs. Fitzsimmons' face went white but her expression didn't change.

"Oh, yes," she said smoothly. "My filigree necklace lost some pearls in all the activity." She reached for the berry.

"Real pearls?" asked Jo.

Mrs. Fitzsimmons bristled. "Of course real pearls! I do not wear inferior jewelry."

"They're belladonna berries," said Dr. Franks. "We believe you may have put them in Colonel Marsh's punch."

Mrs. Fitzsimmons hand flew to her throat, and she looked swiftly at the policemen.

"Why on earth would I do that?"

Jo pointed up to the painting on the wall. "Because of Banáras. Your husband—"

"I very much resent this, young woman!" Mrs. Fitzsimmons interrupted. "How dare you!"

Jo held out her hand.

"I apologize," she said. "We must have been mistaken. Allow me to return the other pearls I found."

Without thinking, Mrs. Fitzsimmons reached out, and Jo grasped her wrist, turning her palm upward. Two of her fingers were stained with dark purple juice.

"And this is the proof," she said, looking over at Sergeant Collins, who nodded to the constable.

"Mrs. Fitzsimmons, I regret to say that I must place you under arrest."

The woman puffed up, red in the face, but then all at once seemed to abandon her fury. She slumped her shoulders and bowed her head as the constable took her arm and led her gently to the door.

As Jo, Jacques, and Bridget carried their boxes out to the cart, Jimmy and Patrick followed.

"That was amazing," said Jimmy. "How did you know it was her? How did you know they weren't pearls? How did you know it wasn't someone else?"

"Miss Harris sees things differently," said Bridget.

"Because she's an artist, I think."

"And a very clever one," said Dr. Franks, shaking Jo's hand in farewell. MacDougall bowed and the two men left, conversing as they went. Patrick and Jimmy said their goodbyes too and went out into the night.

"Poor Colonel Marsh," said Jo. "He did his best to save the women and children. Obviously he couldn't save everyone."

"From what I've heard about the mutiny, he was lucky to save anyone at all," said Jacques, closing the back of the van.

"Would it be horrid to say I'm glad she poisoned the punch, and not my desserts?" said Bridget. "Can you imagine if someone got a poisoned tart by mistake?"

Jo shook her head ruefully. "Especially if it were Mrs. Beeton or her daughter."

Jacques smiled. "You'd have to change the name to Cakes of Destruction."

"Thank goodness," said Jo. "Let's go home."

Lisa M. Lane writes historical mysteries, literary fiction, historical romance, and academic works. After several decades as a college history instructor and online teaching maven, she turned her hand to putting flesh on the bones of the historical past. She lives in San Diego with her husband David, an artist-woodworker, and their cat Sabrina.

The Tommy Jones Mysteries
Murder at Old St. Thomas's
Murder on the Pneumatic Railway
Murder at an Exhibition

Literary Fiction
Before the Time Machine

Victorian Romance
A Heart Purloined

Academic/Reference
H. G. Wells on Science Education, 1886-1897

For more information and to subscribe to the mailing list, please visit https://grousablebooks.com.

www.ingramcontent.com/pod-product-compliance
Lightning Source LLC
Chambersburg PA
CBHW020657010826
48969CB00013B/2418